t...

and
The Pajama Girls

The Case of the Missing Ballet Slippers

Written by MICHELLE WALLACH

Illustrated by JENNY MATTHESON

For Hanna, till we meet
For Emma and Isabel, My Pajama Girls
M.W.

ISBN: 1451544332
ISBN-13: 9781451544336

Library of Congress Control Number: 2010906330

CONTENTS

1

HOME FROM SCHOOL

On Monday, Hanna Taylor rushed home from school. The school bus dropped her off at the corner of her street. She walked home quickly.

As she walked up the front path to her house, she looked at her watch. It was already 3:20 p.m. Every Thursday she went to ballet class. She had to be at her ballet class by 3:45 p.m. She had no time to waste.

Mrs. Taylor opened the front door. "Hi Hanna," she said.

"Hi Mom," said Hanna as she rushed past her Mom to go upstairs to her bedroom. "I'll be ready in just a minute," Hanna called back to her Mom as she ran up the stairs.

In her room, Hanna quickly changed into her ballet clothes. Now all she needed to do was grab her ballet slippers and hurry to class. She ran downstairs.

Sam, their dog, was sitting at the bottom of the steps waiting to greet Hanna with a few licks.

"Hi Sam," Hanna said to him as she leaned down to pet him.

"Let's go, Hanna," called Mrs. Taylor.

"Bye Sam," said Hanna as she got up to leave. "I'll see you later."

Hanna always left her ballet slippers by the bench at the front door. She ran over to the bench to grab them. But this time, the ballet slippers were not where she had left them.

What was she to do? It was already 3:30 p.m. Ballet class was going to start in just fifteen minutes.

Hanna thought about Miss Helen, her ballet instructor. Miss Helen insisted that the students be on time for class. Hanna could not be late for class.

Mrs. Taylor called for her again, "Sweetheart, we need to leave for class if you are going to be on time."

"I'm coming Mom," answered Hanna.

She looked around and thought once more about where she might have left her ballet slippers. No luck. Today, she would have to go to class without her ballet slippers.

Mrs. Taylor had already gone outside to the car. Hanna ran outside to meet Mrs. Taylor. She got into the car with Mrs. Taylor and they drove to class.

Hanna kept trying to figure out where she may have left her ballet slippers. After they drove for a few minutes, Hanna turned to Mrs. Taylor and asked, "Mom, have you seen my ballet slippers?"

"No dear, I have not," answered Mrs. Taylor.

"Well, I was sure that I had left them by the bench but when I went to get them, they were not there," said Hanna.

"I'm sure you will find them later," said Mrs. Taylor as they pulled up to the ballet school. "Now go to your class and have fun."

Hanna couldn't imagine how she was going to have fun. She was too worried about where her ballet slippers might be. She was even more worried about what Miss Helen would say.

Hanna jumped out of the car and ran into the building. She quickly pulled open the door and rushed up the stairs to her classroom.

Meanwhile, Mrs. Taylor parked the car. "Where could those ballet slippers be?" Mrs. Taylor wondered. She knew that Hanna always left her ballet slippers in the same place next to the bench. She was surprised that they were not there.

"Well there is nothing I can do about it now," thought Mrs. Taylor as she sat in the parking lot waiting for Hanna. The class would last one hour.

Mrs. Taylor waited in the parking lot. She reached into her purse and took out her book. She always carried a book with her so she would have something to read while she waited.

Mrs. Taylor had just settled into reading her book when her cell phone rang. The ring startled her. She answered the cell phone.

"Hello," said Mrs. Taylor.

"Hi. This is Marjorie," the caller said.

Marjorie Fisher was the Taylor family's next-door neighbor. She was an elderly woman. Her husband died last year and her kids lived in another state. Now she lived alone. The Taylor family was always looking after her and trying to help her.

"Hi, Marjorie," said Mrs. Taylor. "How nice to hear from you. I do hope you are enjoying this beautiful day."

"Not exactly," said Marjorie. "I am not feeling too well."

"What's wrong?" Mrs. Taylor asked.

"I just have a headache," said Marjorie. "I am sure I will feel better by the morning."

"Oh, I am so sorry to hear that," said Mrs. Taylor. "Is there anything I can do to help you?"

"Well actually, you can," said Marjorie. "That's why I called. I know that you go to the grocery store every Thursday. I need a few items and I was hoping that you could pick them up for me so I don't have to go out."

"Oh, that's no problem at all," said Mrs. Taylor. "Just tell me what you need and I will be happy to help. Give me a moment so I can write down what you need."

Mrs. Taylor opened her purse again. This time she took out a pad and a pen. Now she was ready to jot down the list of items from Marjorie.

"Okay," said Mrs. Taylor. "I have my pen and I am ready to jot down your list."

"I just need a few items," said Marjorie. "I need butter, eggs, milk, bread and some American cheese."

"Anything else?" asked Mrs. Taylor.

"No, I think that's good," said Marjorie.

"Great," said Mrs. Taylor. "Are you sure there is nothing else I can do to help you?"

"No dear," said Marjorie. "But thank you for asking. Now that I know you are going to pick up my groceries, I can go take a nap. I know that will help me feel better."

"Great," said Mrs. Taylor. "I'll stop by around seven to drop off the groceries."

"See you later," said Marjorie.

"Good-bye," said Mrs. Taylor.

Mrs. Taylor put her cell phone away. She enjoyed the quiet for a moment. Then she took out her book again and began to read. She would have plenty of time to read while she waited for Hanna's ballet class to end.

THE BALLET CLASS

Hanna's heart began to race as she climbed the stairs to her ballet class. She had been so worried about where her ballet slippers might be that she hadn't realized it was almost time for class to begin. She might be late.

Hanna's worries quickly disappeared when she walked into the ballet class and saw her friends, Emma and Isabel. The girls had been best friends since their very first ballet class together. Long ago, Hanna's Nana nicknamed them "The

Pajama Girls" because they often had sleepovers at each other's houses.

Hanna felt much better as soon as she saw her friends. "Hi," she said to Emma and Isabel. "I thought I might be late."

"You're never late," said Isabel surprised.

"We were worried that you weren't coming today," said Emma.

"And then how would you practice for the big show on Saturday?" said Isabel.

"We could never perform the show without you," added Emma.

"Don't worry, I'm here," said Hanna. "I wouldn't let you two down."

Still her friends could she that she was worried.

"Hanna, what's wrong?" asked Isabel.

"Oh nothing," replied Hanna. But the friends knew something was wrong. Hanna was not acting like herself.

"It's time for class to begin," said Emma. "Let's go inside."

Miss Helen began the class by taking attendance to make sure that all of the girls were there. There were seven girls in the class and they were all there. Besides the three friends, there was Rosie, Marguerite, Cassie and Ali. All of the girls had been taking ballet classes together for years.

While she was taking attendance, Miss Helen noticed that Hanna was not wearing her ballet slippers. When she was done with attendance, Miss Helen turned to Hanna and asked, "Where are your ballet slippers?" Now, Hanna was nervous.

Emma and Isabel looked at each other. Now they knew why Hanna had looked so worried. They wanted to help their friend but they hadn't noticed that Hanna wasn't wearing her ballet slippers. They were confused. They both wondered, "Why isn't Hanna wearing her ballet slippers?"

"I'm sorry, Miss Helen, but I could not find them and I did not want to be late to class," Hanna answered.

"Well that's okay for class today," said Miss Helen. "But it will not be okay for the show on Saturday. You MUST have you ballet slippers for our big show on Saturday or you cannot be in the show."

"No problem," replied Hanna. "I promise I will have my ballet slippers for Saturday."

Now all of the girls were worried that Hanna would not be able to find her ballet slippers by Saturday. They knew how sad Hanna would be if she missed the show on Saturday. Also, they were upset because they realized how difficult it would be for them to perform the show without Hanna. The girls had been dancing and performing together for six years. They all relied upon each other. They worked as a team. The girls could not imagine performing the show without a member of the team.

Hanna tried her best to focus on the class. The girls did a wonderful job rehearsing for Saturday's performance. Hanna performed her solo beautifully even in her bare feet. She was so excited to

be performing a solo in the performance. She imagined that her solo would be so much more beautiful performed with her ballet slippers.

When the class ended, Miss Helen walked over to Hanna. "You did a great job today," she told Hanna. "Don't look so worried. I am sure you will find your ballet slippers in time for Saturday's performance."

"I sure hope so," said Hanna.

"Well you looked great out there today even without your ballet slippers," said Miss Helen.

"Thanks," replied Hanna.

"Try to have a good night," said Miss Helen as she walked toward her office.

Hanna walked outside the classroom to the waiting area where Emma and Isabel were taking off their ballet slippers. Their pink satin ballet slippers looked so beautiful. As she watched them, Hanna felt sad that she was not taking off her ballet slippers right now. Instead, Hanna quickly slipped her sneakers on her feet and she was ready to go.

Silently, the girls walked downstairs and waved goodbye to each other. Mrs. Taylor was waiting outside in the car. She had just noticed that class had ended and she was putting away her book. She glanced up from her pocketbook and saw Hanna. As soon as Mrs. Taylor saw her, she knew something was wrong.

"Hanna, why do you look so worried?" asked Mrs. Taylor.

"Mom, Miss Helen said that if I cannot find my ballet slippers, I will not be able to perform in the show on Saturday," said Hanna.

"Oh, I see," said Mrs. Taylor.

"I don't understand Mom," said Hanna. "I always take such good care of my ballet slippers. How could I have lost them?"

"Sweetheart, like I told you before, I am sure you will find them," replied Mrs. Taylor.

Hanna was not so sure. All class she had thought about where the slippers might be hiding. In her mind, she had gone through every room in her house and she could not come up with any ideas.

Trying to change the subject, Mrs. Taylor asked, "How was your solo rehearsal?"

"Not so great without my ballet slippers," answered Hanna.

"Are you sure about that?" asked Mrs. Taylor.

"Well, it was good but not as good as it could have been if I had my ballet slippers," answered Hanna.

"That sounds more like it," said Mrs. Taylor, "I am sure you did a wonderful job."

"Miss Helen said I did a wonderful job," said Hanna.

"I knew it," said Mrs. Taylor. "You've spent a lot of time practicing that solo. I knew it would be beautiful with or without ballet slippers."

"Mom, I can't stop thinking about my ballet slippers," said Hanna.

"Well, no time to think about it now," said Mrs. Taylor. "We have to meet your dad and your brother at the restaurant for dinner."

"Oh no, Mom," said Hanna. "I had hoped to go home and look for my ballet slippers."

"They'll be plenty of time for that later dear," said Mrs. Taylor. "Now it's time for dinner."

As they drove to the restaurant Hanna continued to think about where her ballet slippers might be. She knew she would never be able to get new ballet slippers in time. Her ballet slippers were special shoes called Pointe shoes. A dancer had to dance for many years before she was able to learn to dance on Pointe shoes. It was a very special privilege.

The dance store did not keep Pointe shoes in stock. New Pointe shoes would have to be ordered. After they arrived, she would have to sew on the ribbons and elastic before they could be worn. And then, she would have to break them in before they could be worn in a performance.

It was already Thursday. Hanna only had two days until Saturday. There was not enough time to get a new pair of Pointe shoes. If Hanna was going to dance in the performance, she would have to find her Pointe shoes.

Suddenly, Hanna heard Mrs. Taylor calling her name. She had become so distracted by the missing shoes that she did not realize that Mrs. Taylor had already parked the car in the restaurant parking lot. Mrs. Taylor was already out of the car and heading toward the restaurant. Hanna jumped up and followed Mrs. Taylor into the restaurant.

3

ETHAN'S BIG GAME

"Hi Hanna! Hi Mom!" Ethan called to them.

He was sitting at a table by the window with Mr. Taylor. The restaurant was very crowded. Hanna and Mrs. Taylor made their way over to the table.

Ethan jumped up and gave Mrs. Taylor a big hug when they got to the table. "We won!" Ethan shouted. "Our team is going to the baseball championships!" Ethan was so excited.

Mr. Taylor explained that the best part was that Ethan had scored the game-winning run. "It was amazing," said Mr. Taylor. "Everyone cheered for Ethan. I was very proud of him."

Then Ethan explained how his team won the game. The team had been down by one run going into the bottom of the ninth inning. When it was Ethan's turn to get up to bat, there were already two boys on bases. He missed the first pitch. But when the second ball came right down the line, Ethan swung and the ball landed in centerfield. By the time the centerfielder got the ball and threw it into the infield, Ethan scored a double. Both boys on base scored and the game ended with Ethan's team ahead by one run.

As soon as the second boy rounded home plate, all of Ethan's teammates rushed him and jumped on him. It was one big celebration. There were big cheers from the parents in the bleachers.

"Wow!" said Hanna. "I can't believe we missed that."

"It was very exciting!" said Mr. Taylor.

"It sounds like I missed a great game," said Mrs. Taylor. "I'm sorry I wasn't able to be there to see you."

"That's okay Mom," said Ethan. "I knew you had to take Hanna to ballet. You would have been real proud."

"I am real proud!" said Mrs. Taylor.

"I'm really proud of you too!" Hanna added.

Ethan's face beamed. It was so nice for him to hear how proud his family was of him. It made him feel great.

Just then the waitress came over to take the order.

"We're not quite ready yet," said Mr. Taylor. "We've been too busy talking."

"No problem," said the waitress. "I'll be back in a few minutes."

"Well, we had better take a look at the menus so we can order," said Mrs. Taylor.

But Ethan and Hanna did not need to look at the menus. They placed the same order every week. They each got a grilled cheese with French fries and a chocolate milkshake. It was their favorite order. Mr. and Mrs. Taylor always encouraged them to order a healthier meal, but not this time. Tonight was a special celebration for Ethan's great game. They let the kids eat whatever they wanted.

After they had ordered, Mr. Taylor turned to Hanna. "How was your ballet class today?" Mr. Taylor asked. "Are you all ready for the big show on Saturday?"

All the talk of Ethan's exciting game had allowed Hanna to forget about her day. But now it all came back to her.

"It wasn't so good, Dad," Hanna replied.

"What happened dear?" Mr. Taylor asked. "You always love your ballet class."

"When I came home after school, I went to get my ballet slippers but they were not where I left them and I had no time to look for them," Hanna said. "So I had to go to class without my ballet slippers. Miss Helen was okay with me not having my ballet slippers for today's class but she said that if I did not have them on Saturday, I could not be in the performance."

"I'm sure you will find them dear," said Mr. Taylor.

"Why does everyone keep saying that?" Hanna said rudely.

"Dear, there is no reason to get rude with your Dad just because he is trying to make you feel better," said Mrs. Taylor.

"Sorry," Hanna said to her Dad.

"I know how well you take care of your ballet slippers Hanna," said Mr. Taylor. "I am sure they have not disappeared."

"I'm not so sure Dad," said Hanna. "In my mind, I keep going through all of the rooms in our house and I have no idea where I might have left them."

"Maybe it will help to be in the house and actually go through the rooms," said Ethan.

"I sure hope so," said Hanna.

"Well, I'll be happy to help you look when we get home," said Ethan.

"Thanks," said Hanna. "That would be very helpful."

"No problem," said Ethan. "I can see how worried you are."

"I have plenty of time to help you too," said Mr. Taylor.

"Me too!" Mrs. Taylor added.

Just then, the food arrived. Once Hanna was drinking her favorite milkshake, she forgot about the missing ballet shoes and simply enjoyed the celebration. After all, it was a great day for Ethan and his baseball team.

"Tell me more about the game," Mrs. Taylor told Ethan.

"After I missed the first pitch, I got really scared," said Ethan.

"I bet you did," said Mrs. Taylor.

"I was afraid we would lose the game and it would all be my fault," said Ethan.

"Well that wouldn't have been the case but I can understand why you would feel that way," said Mr. Taylor. "You can never forget that you are working on a team and everyone plays a part. It is never one person's fault if you win or lose the game."

"I know Dad but I would have felt like I had let down my fellow teammates if I didn't make the runs to win the game," said Ethan.

"Sort of how I will feel if I am not able to perform in Saturday's show and I let down my fellow classmates," said Hanna.

"I guess so," said Mr. Taylor.

"Wow, you must be feeling terrible," said Ethan.

"You can say that," said Hanna.

"Hanna, you are already assuming that we will not find those ballet slippers and I will not accept that," said Mrs. Taylor. "We will all work hard and we will find those ballet slippers."

"I agree," said Mr. Taylor. "We need to think more positively."

"Exactly," said Mrs. Taylor. "When Ethan got up to bat, he did not assume that he was going to strike out and cause the team to lose the game. No way. He assumed he was going to get a hit and win the game."

"And that's what you need to do Hanna," said Mr. Taylor. "You need to be convinced that we are going to find those ballet slippers and that you are going to put on your best performance yet."

"Okay," said Hanna. "I'll try to think more positively."

"Great," agreed Mr. and Mrs. Taylor as they looked at each other.

The waitress came by the table and dropped off the check. Mr. Taylor quickly paid the bill. Now they were ready to leave the restaurant.

Mrs. Taylor had to go to the grocery store to get some milk and juice for tomorrow's breakfast. Ethan volunteered to help her since he had no homework to do. Hanna went straight home with Mr. Taylor so she could get her homework done and begin the search for her ballet slippers.

TIME FOR HOMEWORK

Mr. Taylor and Hanna walked toward the car. As they got into the car, Hanna said, "Dad, I feel very nervous about my missing ballet shoes."

"Sweetheart, remember to just keep thinking positively," said Mr. Taylor. "We will all work together and we will find them."

"I would feel better if I had some idea where I had left them but I don't," said Hanna. "I always leave them in the same place on the front hall bench. If they are not where I leave them every time, I have no idea where to begin," continued Hanna.

"Well, I think a good place to begin might be in your bedroom," said Mr. Taylor. "Maybe you were distracted when you came home from your last ballet class and brought them upstairs with you into your bedroom."

"Great idea," said Hanna, "I hadn't thought about the possibility that I had brought them upstairs with me."

Hanna thought about her bedroom. There were many places the ballet slippers could be hiding in there. Maybe Mr. Taylor was right and they would find them right away.

"Sweetheart, your ballet slippers did not disappear. I am confident that we will find them with plenty of time for you to wear them to Saturday's performance," said Mr. Taylor.

"I wish I was as confident as you Dad," said Hanna.

Hanna wondered how he could be so sure that they would find the ballet slippers. But Mr. Taylor's confidence made Hanna feel better. She relaxed and they drove the rest of the trip in silence.

When they pulled up in the driveway, Mr. Taylor looked at Hanna and said, "First things first, dear. Go and get your homework done. Then, when Mom and Ethan get home, we will all search for your ballet slippers together."

"Dad, please help me look for the ballet slippers first," said Hanna. "I do not think I will be able to concentrate on my homework until I find my ballet slippers."

"Hanna, please get your homework done first," replied Mr. Taylor. "Your homework is due tomorrow and we still have two days to find your ballet slippers."

Hanna interrupted, "Please Dad."

"Sorry dear," Mr. Taylor said firmly. "Homework first."

He knew Hanna had to get her homework done before they all began the search for the shoes together. Secretly, Mr. Taylor was afraid it might take all night to find the shoes and he did not want Hanna to go to school without her homework tomorrow. That would mean even more trouble.

So Hanna headed straight to her room, sat down at her desk and began her work. Sam lay at her feet and kept her company while she did her homework. Every once in a while, she peeked her head up from her desk to look around her room for the ballet shoes. She did not see them anywhere.

Just then, the phone rang. Hanna hoped it was Mrs. Taylor saying that she was just about home. "Hello," Hanna answered the phone.

"Hi, it's Cassie," she said. "I'm at my house doing homework with Ali."

"Hi," replied Hanna.

"We were just talking about ballet class. We felt awful that you did not have your ballets slippers today and we wanted to see if you had found them," said Cassie.

"We really feel awful for you," added Ali.

"Not yet," said Hanna.

"Well, if there is anything we can do to help you, please know that all you have to do is ask," said Cassie.

"Thanks for thinking about me," said Hanna.

"You're our friend," said Ali. "That's what friends are for."

"Right now I just have to finish my homework so I can search for my ballet slippers when my Mom gets home," replied Hanna.

"Well, get back to your homework," said Cassie. "We really do have a lot of homework tonight."

"We'll see you in school tomorrow," added Ali.

"Bye," said Hanna as she hung up the phone.

Hanna sat back for a moment. She thought about how lucky she was to have such a wonderful family and friends who were all so willing to help her look for her missing ballet slippers.

Quickly, Hanna got back to her homework. She had to do a lot of Math homework and she had to study for a quiz in Italian tomorrow.

The phone rang again. This time it was Rosie. She and Marguerite were doing their homework together and they wondered if she had found her ballet slippers. Hanna explained that she had not even had a chance to start looking for them yet.

"Oh, no," said Rosie. "You must still be so worried."

"Not really," said Hanna. "I know I am going to find them. Right now, I just have to get my homework done so that I can start the search for the missing ballet slippers."

"Oh, great," said Rosie. "Marguerite and I kept thinking about you while we were doing our homework and we did not want you to feel like you were alone in this search so if you need any help, please don't hesitate to ask."

"Thanks," said Hanna. "But I think I have enough help right now."

"Oh, great," said Marguerite. "We feel so much better to hear you are feeling better now. You looked so sad in ballet class today."

"My family really helped me feel better," said Hanna.

"Great," said Rosie. "But please know you can always call on us to help you too."

"Thanks again," said Hanna. "I'll see you in school tomorrow."

"Bye," said Rosie.

"Bye," said Hanna.

Finally, Hanna was ready to get her Math homework done. But the phone rang again.

"I will never get my homework done," thought Hanna.

"Hi, it's Emma," the voice answered.

"Hi, Emma," said Hanna. "I'm trying to get my homework done but I can't seem to get off the phone."

"Oh, great," said Emma. "So you already found your ballet slippers?"

"Oh, no, not yet" said Hanna. "But everyone is so kind they just keep calling to see how I am doing and if I have found my ballet slippers."

"Oh, I see," said Emma.

"First, I got a call from Cassie and Ali," said Hanna. "Then, I got a call from Rosie and Marguerite. And now you are calling me."

"Well, me and Isabel," said Emma. "We are at my house doing our homework together and we could not stop thinking about how sad you seemed in class today so we wanted to call and see how you were doing."

"Well, now that everyone has called me and really shown me how much they care about me, I'm doing great," said Hanna.

"You're feeling great even though you haven't yet found your ballet slippers?" questioned Emma.

"That's right," said Hanna. "I feel great knowing how many people care and are concerned about me."

"Oh, Hanna," said Emma. "It's so great to just hear your voice sounding so happy. We were very worried about you today."

"I'm okay now," said Hanna. "And as soon as Mom and Ethan get home from the grocery store, we are going to look for my ballet slippers together."

"Oh, great!" said Emma.

"But Mom said I can't start looking for my ballet slippers until I finish my homework," said Hanna. "I had better get back to my homework so that I can begin the search for my ballet slippers at some point tonight."

"Okay," said Emma, "Get working and we will see you in school in the morning."

"Bye," said Hanna.

"Bye," said Emma.

Hanna got right to work on her homework. She felt much better now and she quickly worked her way through it all. She couldn't wait for Mrs. Taylor and Ethan to get home and begin the search with her.

5

AT THE GROCERY STORE

Meanwhile, Mrs. Taylor and Ethan drove to the grocery store.

"I have a list of a few items I need to buy for Mrs. Fisher," said Mrs. Taylor. "I was hoping that you could go and grab those items while I pick out the items we need."

"No problem, Mom," said Ethan.

"I was hoping it would help us get finished quickly so that we could get home and help Hanna look for her ballet shoes," continued Mrs. Taylor.

"Hanna looked very upset," said Ethan.

"I know," said Mrs. Taylor. "She has been upset all day. That's why we need to get home quickly."

When they arrived at the grocery store, they each took a shopping cart from the parking lot. They went into the store together and then headed in their separate directions to pick up their items.

Ethan thought about Mrs. Fisher. She had been their next-door neighbor ever since he could remember. She had always been so good to him. He was sad that she was growing older now and sometimes needed their help. But it always made him feel good to be able to help her.

Ethan headed straight to the dairy aisle. He looked down at the list and saw "American cheese." He thought about Mrs. Fisher and the yummy American cheese sandwiches she used to make for him when he was a little boy. Then, he remembered her husband, Jack, who died last year. Mrs. Fisher would make American cheese sandwiches for the two of them. While she made the sandwiches, Mr. Fisher made the lemonade. Then, Mr. Fisher and Ethan would sit on the Fishers' porch, eating their lunch and talking about baseball. Mr. Fisher was a big baseball fan. Ethan would have been so excited to share the story of today's game with Mr. Fisher. He would have been so proud of Ethan. Suddenly, Ethan felt sad. He really missed Mr. Fisher.

Just then, Ethan felt a pat on his back. He turned around and saw Joe Lewis, the Taylors' new neighbor, together with his two young boys, Matt and Mark. The Lewis family recently moved in across the street. Ethan had seen Mr. Lewis playing catch with the boys in their yard.

"Sorry I startled you," said Mr. Lewis.

"Oh, no, I was so deep in thought when you came along that I didn't even notice you," Ethan replied.

"Well, I'm sorry to interrupt your thoughts but I had to come over to congratulate you on your game tonight," said Mr. Lewis.

"You saw my game?" asked Ethan.

"Well, I have heard so many wonderful stories about you so I kept telling my wife that I had to go down to the ball field to watch you play," said Mr. Lewis. "And then tonight, I finally found some time so I ran down to the field just in time to see your play. You were amazing!"

"Wow, you really came down to the ball field to see my game?" asked Ethan.

"Of course I did," said Mr. Lewis. "You have quite the reputation young man and you certainly lived up to it tonight."

"Thanks," replied Ethan.

"You really made me proud!" said Mr. Lewis. "I was telling everyone around me that I know you."

"I don't know what to say," replied Ethan. "Thank you so much, Mr. Lewis."

"No, thank you, son," said Mr. Lewis. "I really enjoyed watching baseball tonight."

"Your welcome," Ethan said to Mr. Lewis. "I really love to play the game."

"Next time, I am going to bring my boys to watch you," said Mr. Lewis. "They will be so impressed at how well you play."

"Definitely, bring them to a game," Ethan replied as he looked at the boys. "I think they would enjoy it. I would love to throw the ball with them some time if they would like."

"I'm sure they would," said Mr. Lewis.

"Great, I look forward to it," said Ethan.

"Well I should pick up my groceries and get home," said Mr. Lewis. "It's getting late."

"Oh no, I did not realize how late it was getting already," said Ethan. "I still have to pick up these groceries for Mrs. Fisher and bring them to her house."

"It is really nice of you to help Mrs. Fisher," said Mr. Lewis.

"Well I can't take the credit," said Ethan. "It was my Mom's idea but I am always happy to help Mrs. Fisher."

"You are a fine young man, Ethan," said Mr. Lewis. "You really make me proud."

"Thanks again," Ethan said as they waved good-bye to each other and went their separate ways to get their groceries.

Ethan could not stop thinking about Mr. Lewis. He had come all the way down to the ball field just to watch him play. No one, besides his family and Mr. Fisher, had ever come down to the ball field to watch him play. He had not realized that he had such a wonderful reputation that Mr. Lewis would be interested in coming to watch him play.

Ethan was feeling really good about his night. He felt good until Mrs. Taylor interrupted his thoughts.

"Ethan, where are Mrs. Fisher's groceries?" questioned Mrs. Taylor. "Your cart is empty."

"Sorry Mom," explained Ethan. "I just saw Mr. Lewis."

Mrs. Taylor interrupted, "I don't suppose that Mr. Lewis picked up Mrs. Fisher's groceries for us."

"No, Mom," Ethan explained. "He came over to tell me that he saw my game tonight and that he was really proud of the way I played the game."

45

Mrs. Taylor realized how good Mr. Lewis' comments had made Ethan feel about himself.

"Well, I'm sorry I missed your game tonight but I am really proud of you too," said Mrs. Taylor.

"Mom, I know you're proud of me," explained Ethan. "You're my Mom. But it's really nice to hear that other people are proud of me too."

"Well they should be. It sounds like you played a wonderful game tonight," said Mrs. Taylor.

"It was a great game Mom but I never thought that anyone would come to see me play," said Ethan.

"Well, I did," said Mrs. Taylor. "Ethan, you are a great baseball player and it's about time you realize that!"

"I think maybe I finally realized that tonight," said Ethan giving Mrs. Taylor a big hug.

"Great," said Mrs. Taylor. "But now its time to get Mrs. Fisher's groceries so we can go home!"

They were already in the dairy aisle, so they grabbed the butter, eggs and milk. Now all they needed was the bread. Ethan quickly ran to the bread aisle while Mrs. Taylor waited with the carts by the checkout counter. When Ethan returned, they took both carts to the checkout. Ethan bagged Mrs. Fisher's items separately so he would be able to take them straight to her house when they got home.

6

THE SEARCH FOR THE SLIPPERS

When Hanna was just about finished with her work, she heard Mrs. Taylor's car pulling into the driveway. She ran to her window and saw Ethan going next door to Mrs. Fisher's house. She wondered why he was going next door instead of coming home right away to help her look for her ballet slippers.

Suddenly, she heard the front door open. She quickly ran downstairs. Sam followed her down the stairs. Mrs. Taylor was carrying in the groceries.

"I could use some help dear," said Mrs. Taylor. "I had to leave some packages in the car."

Just then, Mr. Taylor came out of his office where he had been working. He looked toward Hanna. "You stay here and help Mom put away the groceries," he said. "I will get the rest of the packages from the car."

"Thanks Dad," said Hanna as Mr. Taylor walked toward the front door.

Mrs. Taylor and Hanna unpacked the grocery bags.

"By the way dear," said Mrs. Taylor. "On the way home from the grocery store, I called Miss Helen and asked her to search the ballet school for your ballet slippers. Maybe you accidentally left them there after class last week."

"Great idea, Mom," said Hanna. "Thanks for thinking of that."

"No problem dear," said Mrs. Taylor. "She said she will search the school and call us after she finishes."

Mr. Taylor walked back into the kitchen with the rest of the groceries. "That's it," said Mr. Taylor. "I got all of the packages out of the car."

"Thanks," said Mrs. Taylor.

When they were just about done, Mr. Taylor said, "I think we are just about finished here."

"Great. If we are done, can I start searching for my ballet slippers?" asked Hanna.

"Sure," said Mrs. Taylor.

"I have a plan. I'm going to begin upstairs. And if I don't find them upstairs, I am going to work my way downstairs," said Hanna.

"Good idea," said Mrs. Taylor.

"Seems like a very organized plan," added Mr. Taylor.

"Thanks, I've been thinking more clearly and I know that my ballet slippers must be somewhere," said Hanna. "I know that if we do a careful search, we will find them."

"Nice to hear you thinking more positively," said Mr. Taylor.

"Well go get started," said Mrs. Taylor. "We'll be right there to help you."

Hanna left the kitchen. Sam followed behind her. Mr. and Mrs. Taylor looked at each other and sighed. All of this talk about missing ballet slippers had exhausted them.

The phone rang. Mr. Taylor answered the phone. "Hello," he said. "Oh, hi, Miss Helen. I see. Well, thank you so much for your help. I will let Hanna know. Okay. Goodbye." Then, Mr. Taylor hung up the phone.

"What did Miss Helen say?" Mrs. Taylor asked.

"She said she searched the school and she could not find the ballet slippers," said Mr. Taylor sadly.

"Oh," said Mrs. Taylor. "I had really hoped that they might show up there. But I guess not."

"Well I had better get upstairs and tell Hanna that Miss Helen called and the ballet slippers were not at the ballet school," said Mr. Taylor. "She'll be so disappointed." Mr. Taylor walked upstairs.

Just as Mr. Taylor went upstairs, Ethan walked in from Mrs. Fisher's house.

"Looks like you already put away all of the groceries. Do you need any more help?" asked Ethan.

"No thanks. All of the groceries are put away here," said Mrs. Taylor. "Was everything okay at Mrs. Fisher's house?"

"Fine, Mom," answered Ethan. "Mrs. Fisher was lying down because she had a bad headache so I told her not to get up and I put all of the groceries away in her refrigerator."

"Great," said Mrs. Taylor.

"I'm really worried about Mrs. Fisher," said Ethan.

"Why dear?" asked Mrs. Taylor.

"I don't think I have ever seen Mrs. Fisher spend an entire day in bed Mom," said Ethan.

Mrs. Taylor saw the worried look on Ethan's face. "Do you think she'll be okay?" he asked.

"Of course she will dear," said Mrs. Taylor. "She just has a headache."

"I'm not so sure Mom," said Ethan.

"Honey, I think you are more worried than you need to be," said Mrs. Taylor. "I spoke to Mrs. Fisher this afternoon and she really sounded fine."

"Then why didn't she get out of bed, Mom?" demanded Ethan.

"Honey I think that you are more nervous than you need to be because Mr. Fisher died last year," said Mrs. Taylor. "Maybe you're afraid something terrible is going to happen to Mrs. Fisher and she'll die too."

Ethan thought about what Mrs. Taylor had said. He had just been thinking about Mr. Fisher. He had really been missing him. Maybe he was afraid that he would lose Mrs. Fisher too. Then what would he do?

55

"Maybe I am more afraid than I realize Mom," said Ethan.

"Its very scary when we lose someone special in our lives," said Mrs. Taylor. "Especially when we lose someone you knew as long as you knew Mr. Fisher."

"And someone who was my biggest fan," said Ethan.

"Well I don't think he was your biggest fan," said Mrs. Taylor.

Ethan looked at Mrs. Taylor.

"I am definitely your biggest fan," said Mrs. Taylor. "I always have been and I always will be."

"Thanks Mom," said Ethan. "I was just talking about Mr. Fisher with Mr. Lewis. I guess it made me feel sad that Mr. Fisher didn't get to see tonight's game. He would have been so excited. It made me miss him a lot. And I guess that made me feel worried about Mrs. Fisher. They were always so good to me."

"Don't worry dear," said Mrs. Taylor. "I'll give her a call first thing tomorrow and make sure she is okay."

"Thanks, Mom," said Ethan. "I knew you would."

"Now I think we need to help your sister look for her ballet slippers," said Mrs. Taylor.

Mr. Taylor came back into the kitchen.

"She still hasn't found them?" asked Ethan.

"Not yet," said Mr. Taylor.

"Let's go," said Mrs. Taylor. "This might be a very long night."

Mrs. Taylor, Mr. Taylor and Ethan walked upstairs and found Hanna. "We're all here to help you," said Ethan.

"And we are not going to give up until we find those ballet slippers so you can be in your show on Saturday," said Mr. Taylor.

"Okay, let's start searching," said Mrs. Taylor.

They broke into groups. Mrs. Taylor and Ethan worked together. Mr. Taylor and Hanna worked together. First, they looked upstairs. Then, they looked downstairs. They went through each room of the house. They even checked the basement.

Then Mrs. Taylor thought Hanna might have left the ballet slippers in Mrs. Taylor's car. So Mrs. Taylor went outside to search her car. But the ballet slippers were not in Mrs. Taylor's car.

Hours later, they were exhausted and they still had not found Hanna's ballet slippers.

"Those ballet slippers are definitely not in this house," concluded Mr. Taylor.

"I agree," said Mrs. Taylor.

"And they are definitely not in Mom's car," said Ethan.

"I agree," said Mr. Taylor.

"I cannot imagine where else they could be," said Hanna.

7

BACK AT SCHOOL

On Friday morning, Mrs. Taylor drove Ethan and Hanna to school. Hanna walked into the building looking as sad as she had the day before when she arrived at her ballet class.

Emma and Isabel spotted her when she walked into the school.

"From the look on your face, I am guessing that you did not find your ballet slippers," said Emma.

"You are guessing correctly," said Hanna.

"What will you do for the show tomorrow?" asked Isabel.

"I guess I may not be able to be in the show tomorrow," said Hanna.

"How could we have a show without you, Hanna?" asked Emma.

"I don't think we have a choice," said Hanna. "My family and I searched my entire house last night and we could not find my ballet slippers."

"Where could they be?" Isabel asked.

"I think this is a case for the Pajama Girls," said Emma.

"Great idea," agreed Isabel.

"I'm not sure the Pajama Girls will be able to help," said Hanna. "My family already searched everywhere."

"We don't have a choice," said Emma.

"None of the girls want to perform in the show without you," said Isabel.

"If the Pajama Girls put their heads together, they will be able to solve this mystery," said Emma.

"I guess it's worth a shot," said Hanna.

Hanna, Emma and Isabel called themselves the Pajama Girls. Ever since they were little girls, they liked to have a sleepover whenever the girls had a problem to solve. They spent the night going over the problem until they found the answer. Working together, the Pajama Girls solved the mystery. Tonight would be no different. The Pajama Girls would examine the mystery of the missing ballet slippers until they found the slippers.

"I'm sure our Moms will agree," said Isabel.

"Me too," said Emma.

"Great," said Isabel. "We'll be over before dinner."

"Thanks for helping me," said Hanna.

"Friends always help friends," said Emma and Isabel at the same time. The girls turned to each other and laughed. Hanna felt better just knowing she had such great friends.

The girls went off to their separate classes agreeing that they would meet at Hanna's house for a sleepover. As Hanna walked to class, she felt much better. She knew the girls would be able to solve the mystery.

As she walked down the hall, the bell rang. Now Hanna was late for Italian.

"Oh no," thought Hanna. "We have a quiz today." Quickly, Hanna raced down the hall and sneaked into her Italian class.

But Mrs. Fina noticed that Hanna was late to class.

"Hanna, class began a few moments ago," said Mrs. Fina. "You almost missed the beginning of the quiz."

"Mi dispiace, Signora Fina," said Hanna.

Excited to hear Hanna say she was sorry in Italian, Mrs. Fina quickly forgave Hanna for being late to class.

"Okay class, now that we are all here, let's begin the quiz," said Mrs. Fina, as she walked around the class handing out the quiz papers to the students.

"Turn the papers over," said Mrs. Fina. "You have 30 minutes to complete the quiz. Good luck."

Hanna turned her paper over. The quiz was on vocabulary words including the names of the animals and the parts of the body. She took a deep breath.

"It's going to be okay," she thought. "I know these."

Hanna finished the quiz quickly. She knew all of the answers. She felt good about how she had done on the quiz. She checked it over and handed it in before the time was up.

When she handed it in, Mrs. Fina pulled her aside.

"Are you okay, Hanna?" asked Mrs. Fina. "You looked very nervous when you came into class and it didn't look like you were nervous about being late to class."

"I am okay," answered Hanna. "Its just that I have lost my ballet slippers and I am so worried that I will not be able to find them before

Saturday's performance. If I cannot find them before the performance, I will not be able to perform in the show."

"No wonder you look so worried my dear," said Mrs. Fina. "I knew it had to be something more than being a few minutes late to class."

"Emma and Isabel have agreed to come to my house and help me look for them," said Hanna.

"That's great, Hanna," said Mrs. Fina. "I know how well you girls work together."

Mrs. Fina had been teaching Italian to the girls for years. She knew them well. The girls had often volunteered to help her teach the younger children during the after-school session. The girls were always so helpful and kind to the younger children. She knew how well the girls worked together. Most important, she knew that if the three girls put their heads together, there was nothing they could not do. She was sure they would find the ballet slippers.

"It's just getting close to the show," said Hanna.

65

"Tell me where you have looked so far," said Mrs. Fina.

"Well, my whole family searched my entire house and we found nothing," said Hanna.

"Are there any other places you searched?" asked Mrs. Fina.

"My Mom searched her car and she found nothing," said Hanna.

"Great," said Mrs. Fina. "Any place else?"

"Miss Helen searched the ballet school and she found nothing," said Hanna.

"So you have already looked in a lot of places – your house, your car, and the ballet school," said Mrs. Fina. "It sounds to me like there are still a lot of other places you can look."

"That's the problem," said Hanna. "How can I possibly search everywhere?"

"Well you don't need to search everywhere," said Mrs. Fina. "You just need to retrace your steps and search any place that you might have gone with your ballet slippers. I am sure you will think of another place where your ballet slippers might be that you have not yet searched."

"It sounds much easier than it is," said Hanna.

"That's for sure," said Mrs. Fina. "Just keep thinking about the places you might have gone that you have not yet searched."

The bell rang. It was time for Hanna to go to her next class.

"Thanks for the help," said Hanna. "I had better get my books and move to my next class before I am late for another class."

"Good luck Hanna!" said Mrs. Fina.

Hanna walked down the hall toward her locker. She saw Ethan standing by her locker. She didn't know why he was there.

"Hey, Sis," said Ethan. "I kept thinking about how sad you looked this morning and I just wanted to come by and say hi."

"Thanks," said Hanna. "I think I have everyone worried about my ballet slippers by now."

"I'm sure you do," said Ethan.

"Emma and Isabel have agreed to sleep over and have The Pajama Girls solve the mystery," said Hanna.

"Great," said Ethan. "When you three work together, you do seem to unravel the mysteries."

"I know," said Hanna. "And Mrs. Fina gave me an idea of retracing my footsteps to try to think of another place where I might have left my ballet slippers."

"Sounds like one Pajama Girl is already on the job," said Ethan.

"I am," said Hanna. "But I can always use my big brother's help!"

"Just ask and you've got it," said Ethan.

"Thanks for being such a great big brother," said Hanna.

Just then, the bell rang. It was time for the next class to begin.

"Oh no," said Hanna. "I'm late again."

"Well I am heading out to lunch," said Ethan.

"I just realized I have a study hall," said Hanna. "Thank goodness I'm not late for another class. But I really should get over there."

"See you after school," said Ethan as he left for lunch.

"Bye," said Hanna.

Hanna went quickly to study hall. She was determined to get all of her homework done in study hall so she could spend the afternoon with her friends looking for the ballet slippers. Hanna got right to work and by the time the bell rang to go to the next class, all of her homework was complete.

The next few classes went quickly. Soon it was the end of the school day. Hanna met Ethan at the front of the building and together they got on the bus to go home.

Hanna fell asleep on the bus. She had not slept much the night before and all of her worrying had exhausted her. Ethan leaned her head on his shoulder so her head would stop bobbing up and down every time the bus stopped.

Ethan was tired too. It had been a long week for him. Now that the school day was over, he was anxious to get home so he could check on Mrs. Fisher. He had been worrying about her all day. He did not like that she wasn't feeling well yesterday.

8

THE SLEEPOVER

Later that afternoon, the girls arrived at Hanna's house for their sleepover. They ran straight upstairs to Hanna's room and set out their sleeping bags. They laid them out in a row, one right next to the other. Sam took turns laying on each of the sleeping bags.

Then, the girls ran back downstairs to get a snack. Sam followed closely behind the girls. Mrs. Taylor was making dinner when the girls came running into the kitchen.

"Hello girls," said Mrs. Taylor.

"Hi, Mrs. Taylor," said Emma.

"Thanks for letting us sleep over tonight, Mrs. Taylor," said Isabel.

"I think I should be the one to say thank you," said Mrs. Taylor. "It's really great that you came to help Hanna find her ballet shoes."

"The Pajama Girls are on the job!" said Isabel.

"The Pajama Girls are always happy to help – especially when one of the Pajama Girls is in trouble," said Emma.

Hanna reached for the refrigerator door.

"What are you looking for dear," said Mrs. Taylor.

"Snacks," said Hanna.

"No snacks now girls," said Mrs. Taylor. "It's time for dinner. I prepared dinner early so you girls would have plenty of time to solve the mystery of the missing ballet slippers."

"That's great, Mom," said Hanna.

Just then, Ethan walked into the kitchen. "Hi everyone!" he said.

"Hi Ethan!" Emma said.

"Hi!" Isabel said.

Mrs. Taylor turned to the girls. "Maybe you girls can set the table in the dining room to help me," said Mrs. Taylor.

"Great!" said the girls at the same time.

After the girls went into the dining room to set the table, Mrs. Taylor turned to Ethan. "How was Mrs. Fisher?" she said.

"Oh, she looks great Mom," said Ethan. "I had been so worried about her all day. As soon as I saw her I felt silly for worrying about her. She said she feels fine again. She was even asking for Hanna. I guess it was just a headache."

"I know how worried you were dear," said Mrs. Taylor. "I am so happy you saw her and she feels much better."

"Me too!" said Ethan.

"You're a good person to think about her," said Mrs. Taylor.

"She really means a lot to me, Mom," said Ethan. "And since Mr. Fisher died, I get very worried about Mrs. Fisher's health."

"I can understand your fear dear," said Mrs. Taylor. "But you also have to remember that Mrs. Fisher is still in very good health and hopefully, she will be with us for many more years. You can't go worrying that she is going to die every time she gets a headache."

"I know Mom," said Ethan. "This made me realize that."

"Great," said Mrs. Taylor. "Now help me get this food on the table. I hear your Dad's car pulling into the driveway and the food is all done so we can all eat dinner now."

"Okay Mom," said Ethan as he carried the food into the dining room. Mrs. Taylor followed him into the dining room and they all sat down to eat.

After dinner, the girls asked to be excused from the table so they could begin the search for the ballet slippers. They quickly ran upstairs to Hanna's room.

"Girls, we have to get to business," said Isabel. "We have less than twenty-four hours to find Hanna's ballet slippers or she will miss our ballet performance."

Emma took out their secret journal where she would write down the clues that would help them solve this mystery. And she took out her magic pen that she would use to write down the clues.

Now that Emma was ready to write down the clues, Isabel began to ask the questions.

"Hanna, who picked you up from ballet class last time?" asked Isabel.

"Mom always picks me up from class," replied Hanna.

"Where did you go after ballet class?" asked Isabel.

"We went to Joe's Diner," said Hanna. "We always go there after ballet class."

"What did you eat for dinner?" asked Isabel.

75

"What does that matter?" replied Hanna.

"Nothing," said Isabel. "I am just curious because I love their grilled cheese sandwich."

"I love the grilled cheese sandwich too!" said Emma.

"Isabel, please keep to the line of questioning," said Hanna. "We really have to find my ballet slippers soon!"

"Okay, okay," said Isabel laughing. "Let's not forget we are here to have fun too."

"I really don't feel like having fun," said Hanna.

"Don't be so blue, Hanna," said Emma. "We are going to find those ballet slippers."

"I know you are both great friends and you really want to help me but I also know that my whole family searched my entire house and we could not find the slippers," said Hanna.

"Great," exclaimed Isabel.

"What could be great about the fact that her family searched the entire house and could not find the ballet slippers?" asked Emma.

"Great," repeated Isabel. "That is our first clue!"

"What is our first clue?" questioned Hanna.

"We know for sure that the shoes are NOT in this house," said Isabel.

"That's true," said Emma. "We have our first clue."

Emma quickly wrote down their first clue in the secret journal.

Pajama Girl Clues
The Ballet Slippers are NOT in the Taylor house.

"Now," said Isabel, "we need to figure out where else you may have left your ballet slippers."

"That is what Mrs. Fina told me to do," said Hanna. "She told me to retrace my footsteps and to think of where else I went that day that I may have left my ballet slippers."

"I think that is the best plan," said Emma.

"Especially since we know they are not in this house," said Isabel.

"Okay, so back to Joe's Diner," said Isabel. "Did you take your ballet slippers into Joe's Diner?"

"No," said Hanna. "I never do that."

"Well did you call them and make sure you didn't take them into the restaurant by mistake and accidentally leave them there," said Isabel.

"No," answered Hanna.

"Well I guess we should do that," said Emma.

The girls were excited. Maybe the mystery would be easily solved and they could enjoy their night together.

Isabel agreed to make the call. She went into the other room to get the phone and called Joe's Diner. The woman at the front desk answered and Isabel asked her if they had found any ballet slippers that someone might have left there. The girl told her that they had not found any ballet slippers. She even checked with the manager who said that they had not found any ballet slippers.

Isabel thanked the woman and hung up the telephone. She walked back into Hanna's room.

"I called Joe's Diner and they do not have the ballet slippers," said Isabel.

The girls were disappointed.

"That's too bad," said Emma.

"Well at least we have our second clue," said Isabel.

"What's that?" asked Emma.

"The ballet slippers are NOT at Joe's Diner," said Isabel. "That's our second clue."

Emma jotted down the second clue in the secret journal.

Pajama Girl Clues

The Ballet Slippers are NOT in the Taylor house.

The Ballet Slippers are NOT at Joe's Diner.

Turning to Hanna, Isabel asked, "Do you remember where you went after Joe's Diner?"

"Home," said Hanna. "Mom and I always come home after Joe's Diner so I can get my homework done."

"But when I spoke to you after ballet class this week, your Mom was at the grocery store," said Emma.

"That's right," said Isabel. "You told us that she and Ethan were at the grocery store."

"That's true," said Hanna. "Usually, we come home after ballet class but sometimes we stop at the grocery store."

"Well, can you remember if you stopped at the grocery store last week?" asked Isabel.

"Yes," said Hanna. "I am sure we stopped at the grocery store because I remember we picked up a few items for Mrs. Fisher next door."

"Well, I guess we had better call the grocery store and see if they found any ballet slippers," said Isabel.

"I'll call this time," said Emma as she walked into the room next door to make the telephone call. Emma was gone for a few minutes.

When Emma came back into Hanna's room, she look disappointed.

"No good," said Emma. "I called the grocery store and they have not found any ballet slippers there. I even spoke to the store manager to make sure and he said that they had not found any ballet slippers at the store."

"Well, now we have our third clue!" said Isabel. "We know that your ballet slippers are NOT at the grocery store."

Emma jotted down the third clue in the secret journal.

"Emma, can you read me the clues?" asked Hanna.

"Sure," said Emma and she began to read the clues.

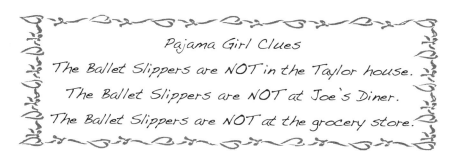

Pajama Girl Clues

The Ballet Slippers are NOT in the Taylor house.

The Ballet Slippers are NOT at Joe's Diner.

The Ballet Slippers are NOT at the grocery store.

"It sounds to me like we know a lot of places where my ballet slippers are NOT but we have no idea where my ballet slippers are," said Hanna.

"That's okay, Hanna," said Emma. "It's called the process of elimination. If we eliminate all of the places where we know the ballet slippers are NOT, eventually we will be left with the one place where the ballet slippers are. Its really very simple."

"I'm happy you think it's simple," said Hanna.

"Now all we need to know is any other place where you might have gone after ballet class last week," said Emma.

"What about your Mom's car?" Isabel asked. "Did you check your Mom's car to see if you left your ballet slippers in her car?"

"No," said Hanna.

Emma and Isabel both jumped up from the floor. The girls were eager to run downstairs and check Mrs. Taylor's car for the ballet slippers. But Hanna stopped them.

"Wait," said Hanna as Isabel was reaching for the doorknob. "My Mom checked her car – twice! That's why I didn't need to check it. She already did it."

"That's too bad," sighed Isabel. "I was so excited. I thought we had solved the mystery."

"Sorry," said Hanna.

"Not yet," said Isabel. "But we will."

"Well I guess I can add another clue to our list of clues," said Emma as she jotted down the fourth clue.

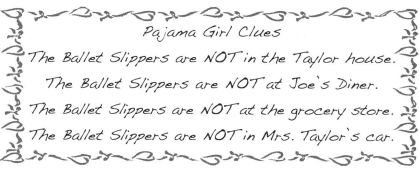

Pajama Girl Clues

The Ballet Slippers are NOT in the Taylor house.

The Ballet Slippers are NOT at Joe's Diner.

The Ballet Slippers are NOT at the grocery store.

The Ballet Slippers are NOT in Mrs. Taylor's car.

"We have a lot of great clues," said Isabel.

"But we still need more," said Emma.

"Okay, back to work," said Isabel. "Hanna, after you came home from the grocery store, where did you go?"

"I went to my room to do my homework like I always do," said Hanna. "I'm sure that the ballet slippers are not in this room because I have searched it over and over again."

"Did you leave the house at all after that?" asked Isabel.

"No," answered Hanna. "I did my homework and got ready for bed."

The girls thought about her answer for a moment.

"If you never left the house again that night and we checked all of the places you went between ballet class and coming home and none of those places have your ballet slippers, I am a little confused," said Isabel.

"We used the process of elimination to narrow down where they might be," said Emma. "But we are not left with any place to search for the slippers."

"It must mean that your ballet slippers have to be at one of the locations already searched and maybe someone just didn't find them," said Isabel.

"Or it means that Hanna has forgotten some place that she went and we haven't searched there," said Emma.

"No, I'm sure I didn't go anyplace else," said Hanna.

"All this work is making me hungry," said Isabel. "Can we go and get some chocolate chip cookies from the kitchen? Mrs. Taylor makes the best chocolate chip cookies."

"I think we could use a break," said Emma.

"Let's go," said Hanna.

Ethan was sitting in the kitchen watching a baseball game on television when the girls came into the room.

"Hi girls," he said. "Any luck finding the ballet slippers?"

"Not yet," said Hanna as she pulled the cookies out of the cabinet.

"I'm sure you girls will figure it out," said Ethan. "I'm heading to my room now."

"Bye," said all of the girls at the same time.

"Oh, Hanna, when I went over to see Mrs. Fisher before, she asked me to tell you she was looking for you," said Ethan as he walked toward the door.

Hanna ran over to Ethan. "You are brilliant," she said and gave him a big kiss on the cheek.

"Thanks," said Ethan looking surprised.

Hanna turned to her friends. "Come on girls, we are going to Mrs. Fisher's house," she exclaimed. The girls all ran past Ethan and headed out the front door. Sam chased after them.

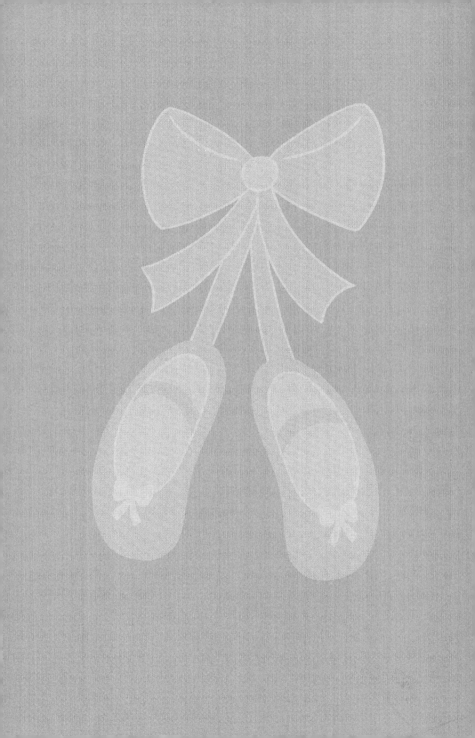

9

A GREAT PERFORMANCE

The girls rang Mrs. Fisher's bell.

While they waited for her to come to the door, Emma asked, "Hanna, why are we here when we still have so much work to do?"

Looking excited, Hanna said, "You'll see."

Just then, Mrs. Fisher came to the door.

"Hi, Mrs. Fisher," said Hanna. "I do hope we are not coming by too late."

"Oh no dear, it's perfect timing," said Mrs. Fisher. "I just finished watching my television shows and I was about to head upstairs to bed."

"Mrs. Fisher, these are my friends, Emma and Isabel," said Hanna. "I believe you have met them before."

"Oh yes, of course," said Mrs. Fisher. "Please do come in."

The girls went into Mrs. Fisher's living room and took a seat.

"I have been waiting for you to come by," said Mrs. Fisher. "I have had your ballet slippers for a whole week now and I was afraid you might need them."

Emma and Isabel looked at each other. Now the girls knew why they had come to visit Mrs. Fisher.

"I have been searching everywhere for my ballet slippers," said Hanna. "I even had my friends help me search for them."

"Oh dear, had you forgotten that I had them?" said Mrs. Fisher.

"Yes, I did," said Hanna. "And I'm afraid I made myself and everyone else a little crazy in the process of searching for them."

Emma and Isabel looked puzzled.

"How did the ballet slippers get here Hanna?" asked Isabel.

"Unfortunately, I forgot that after we came home from the grocery store, I went over to Mrs. Fisher's house to bring her the groceries we had picked up for her," said Hanna. Mrs. Fisher was outside pruning her roses and I began to talk to her. I asked her for some advice on how to sew my ribbons more tightly on my ballet slippers because the thread seemed to be stretching away from the slipper," said Hanna.

"Why did you think that Mrs. Fisher would know how to do that?" asked Isabel.

"Because I was a principal dancer with the City Ballet when I was a young lady," said Mrs. Fisher. "I've had a lot of experience sewing ribbons on my Pointe shoes."

Emma and Isabel both looked surprised. "We had no idea," said Emma.

"Oh yes, when I was a young lady, all I wanted to do was dance," said Mrs. Fisher. "My parents didn't know what to do with me so they put me in lots of dance classes. Eventually, I became a very talented ballerina. I danced with the City Ballet for many years."

"Can you please show my friends your memory book with all of the photos of you dancing with the City Ballet?" asked Hanna.

"Of course, I would love to show it to them," said Mrs. Fisher. Then she walked into the next room to grab the book.

"Mrs. Fisher is a living piece of dance history," said Hanna to her friends.

Mrs. Fisher took a seat in her chair and opened her memory book for the girls to see. The girls gathered around Mrs. Fisher and stared in amazement. There were pictures of Mrs. Fisher as a young girl, dressed in full costume, dancing on Pointe on the stage at City Theatre.

"These photos are wonderful," said Isabel.

"Thank you," said Mrs. Fisher. "I don't take them out very much anymore. My husband used to like to look at them every day before he passed away. He said it made him happy to think of our younger days and all of the wonderful experiences we had had in our lives."

"You must miss him so much," said Hanna.

"I do," said Mrs. Fisher. "But I also realize how lucky I am to have such wonderful neighbors who take such good care of me."

"Wait," said Isabel. "You never explained how Hanna's ballet slippers got into your house."

"Oh, right," said Hanna. "Well I was asking Mrs. Fisher for advice and she said that she would be more than happy to sew them on for me herself."

"So I took the ballet slippers from Hanna," said Mrs. Fisher. "And I sewed the ribbons on the next day. But then you never came back for the ballet slippers. On the day of your class, I meant to bring them over to you but I had such an awful headache, I was stuck in bed all day so I never had a chance to bring them to you."

"And I forgot they were here," said Hanna smiling at Mrs. Fisher. "I only remembered when Ethan told me that you were looking for me."

"I think you'll be very happy with the ribbons," said Mrs. Fisher handing the ballet slippers to Hanna.

"I'm sure I will," said Hanna. "It's not everyday that a professional ballerina sews my ribbons on for me."

"It was my pleasure," said Mrs. Fisher. "It brought back many great memories."

"Well, we had better get home and get some sleep so that we will be ready for our performance tomorrow," said Hanna. "And we do need to let you get your rest as well."

Mrs. Fisher walked the girls to the door. "Have a good night girls," said Mrs. Fisher. "I will see you all at the performance tomorrow."

Hanna looked surprised. "You're coming?" she asked.

"You couldn't keep me away," said Mrs. Fisher.

"Great," said Hanna.

"That's really great," said Isabel, "I can't wait to tell the other girls that real professional ballerina will be sitting in the audience watching our performance."

"They will be so excited," said Emma.

"Good night girls," said Mrs. Fisher.

"Good night Mrs. Fisher," said the girls as they walked back to Hanna's house.

"We'll see you tomorrow," Hanna called back to her.

When they girls got back to Hanna's house, they went straight upstairs to go to bed so they could get enough sleep to be ready for tomorrow's performance. They knew that a professional ballerina would be watching their performance and they were very excited to dance for her. Tomorrow was going to be a great day!

Hanna snuggled up in her sleeping bag. She laid her ballet slippers next to her in the sleeping bag. She wanted them to stay right next to her. She vowed never to misplace them again.

Before they turned out the lights, Emma put the last clue in the secret journal.

Pajama Girl Clues

The Ballet Slippers are NOT in the Taylor house.

The Ballet Slippers are NOT at Joe's Diner.

The Ballet Slippers are NOT at the grocery store.

The Ballet Slippers are NOT in Mrs. Taylor's car.

The Ballet Slippers ARE at Mrs. Fisher's house.

The Pajama Girls did it again!